For my dive buddy and our two fish kids.

And Mum, thanks for everything.

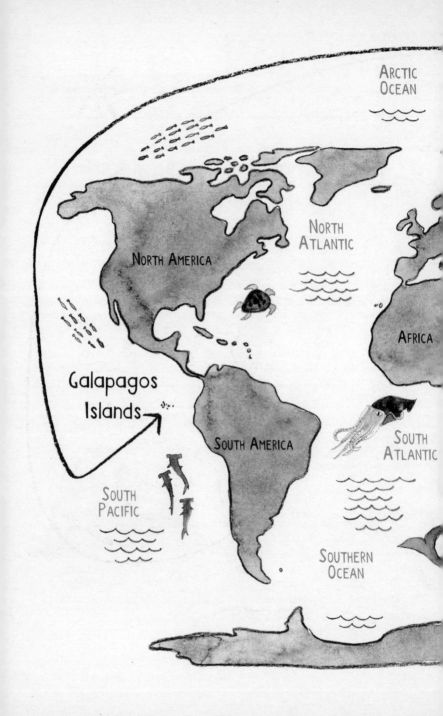

ARCTIC
OCEAN

NORTH
ATLANTIC

NORTH AMERICA

AFRICA

Galapagos
Islands

SOUTH AMERICA

SOUTH
ATLANTIC

SOUTH
PACIFIC

SOUTHERN
OCEAN

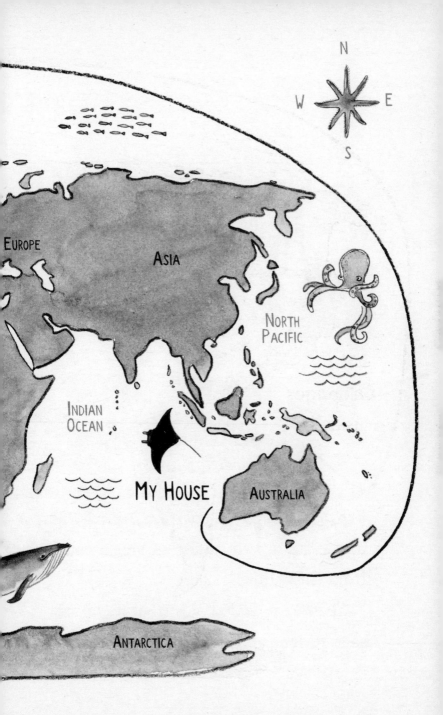

CHAPTER 1

Fishy Family

"PFFT!"

I spat salt water all over the deck. I was like a human fountain! A giggle came from the skipper's cabin.

"YOU!" I yelled, then dragged my salty tongue across my sleeve. "Yuck!"

That was the second time Emely had filled my drink bottle with seawater. I had no idea why she kept doing that. I hadn't done ANYTHING to her. I didn't even know her.

We had been on the boat for three days. Mum and Dad had dragged me out here on their new work project – to collect more weird sea creatures.

"Climate change is a very serious issue," said Dad. "The world's oceans are warmer now than they've been in fifty years."

"That's a good thing," I said. "It's always way too cold in the ocean for me. Brrrrr." He shot me one of his disappointed Dad looks, like the time I got caught sneaking my dinner to the cat. How was I to know crayfish was so

expensive? Tasted like rotten chicken to me.

We were in a place called the Galapagos Islands, a world away from home and my friends.

Dad is a marine biologist, which is a fancy name for someone who stares at fish a lot. Mum is an underwater photographer. We have so many pictures of fish at our house, there's not a speck of white wall left. Fishy eyes stare at me from every room. Barracuda watch me eat, whales watch me sleep ... and penguins watch me poop!

When people come to visit they think they ARE under water. Or in a museum. We have bottles of freaky old fish on every shelf. Most people have a smart TV in their family room. We have a

DUMB flounder stuck to the wall.

It totally creeps out my friends.

I emptied my bottle, tipping the rest of the seawater overboard. A cloud of bubbles boiled on the ocean surface, and a black alien-looking creature emerged through the middle. Its breathing sounded like Darth Vader.

CHAPTER 2

Endangered Cucumbers

The sea alien turned and looked straight at me. It reached up one arm ... then it waved.

"Hi, Bodhi," it said.

"Hey, Dad," I replied. He handed me his catch bag and I pulled it aboard. There were three long sluggy things inside. "Eeeuw, what are those?" I asked, poking at one through the mesh.

Dad pulled the dive reg out of his mouth.

"*Isostichopus fuscus*," he said.

"Octopus whatsits?" I asked.

"*Isostichopus fuscus* – Galapagos sea cucumber."

The skipper helped Dad and his gear out of the water.

"Aren't they amazing?" said Dad. He reached into his catch bag and pulled out the biggest. "Take a look at this beauty," he said, holding it up like a prized sausage at the Royal Show.

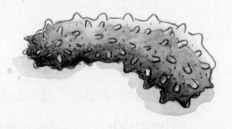

"Your dinner," said the skipper.

"What? That's disgusting!" A tiny bit

of spew jumped up the back of my throat.

"No, no," said Dad. "These are my test specimens. Although they are called sea cucumbers, they're not fruit or vegetables."

"But you CAN eat them," said the skipper.

"Gross!" I said.

Dad went on to explain how they are actually important animals. Something about balancing the ocean, blah blah blah ... and eating fish poop! Basically, sea cucumbers are the vacuum cleaners of the sea.

"Are they tasty?" asked Emely.

"I've never tried them," said Dad. "But they are considered a delicacy in certain countries. Some people even believe sea cucumbers have special healing powers. That's why they've been overfished. Now they are an endangered species."

"That doesn't stop the poachers," said the skipper. "Three men snuck out here at night. Filled their boat."

"They're probably in prison now," said Dad.

"Quick! You'd better throw those back," said the skipper, smirking.

Dad assured us it was okay for him to take a few – only for scientific testing.

"Could you put them in the fridge, please, Emely?" asked Dad. "On the shelf above the jellies."

"Sure," said the skipper's daughter, wiggling the slugs in my face.

"Wait until you see your mum's shark pics," said Dad.

"Sharks?" I asked with a gulp. "Um, Dad, where *is* Mum?"

"Hmmm, she was right behind me," said Dad.

Fish Kid Facts

SEA CUCUMBERS

Breathe through their **anus**.

Are related to **starfish** and **sea urchins**.

Eat **algae, plankton** and **decaying matter** on the sea floor.

Favourite dessert is **fish poo!**

In defence, can expel their **toxic guts** out of their anus, then grow them back again.

Don't have **brains!**

CHAPTER 3

Snack Attack

"Now *that* is a shark," said Mum, flicking through her photos. "Look, Bodhi, Dad is in this shot too." I leaned over Mum's shoulder to see the screen.

Dad looked like a puny little baitfish. The shark was a monster.

"Whoa!" I said. "It could have swallowed you whole!"

You see? My parents are totally nuts.

Who else takes selfies with man-eating sharks?

Emely brought morning tea over to the table. "Oh, thanks Emely," said Mum. "She's such a nice girl, isn't she?" Emely raised one eyebrow and smiled at me. I frowned back. My tongue was still salty after her dirty little prank.

"And a great cook, too," said Dad.

I nibbled at the squashed banana fritter ... it was actually pretty good. Next, I took a cautious sip from my cup. No seawater this time – just juice. Maybe she didn't hate me after all.

Once we were done, Mum fished my mask and flippers out of the plastic dive tub.

"Come for a snorkel, Bodhi."

"Ahhh, I don't know..." I said.

Being in the ocean gave me the shivers. Not just the freeze-your-bones shivers, but the *oh-far-out-what's-about-to-eat-me?* shivers.

"There's a very special creature that I want you to see," said Mum. "This is the only place in the entire world it can be found!"

I stretched the mask onto the

top of my head, then began to pull on my wetsuit. It stank.

I hadn't used it in ages.

"We actually saw some of these prehistoric-looking guys yesterday," she said.

"And you saw a SHARK today!" I reminded her.

"Yes!" said Mum. "She was fabulous." I stopped pulling up my wetsuit.

"Oh come on, my little fish," Mum said. "The best way to overcome a fear of sharks is to meet one!" I shot her a sideways look.

"They're more afraid of us than we are of them," said Dad. He spat into his mask and rubbed the spit around with his finger.

"So, are you coming?"

Fish Kid Facts

GALAPAGOS SHARKS

Are not only found around the **Galapagos Islands**, but in patches all over the world.

Prefer **warmer** waters.

Grow to approximately **3 metres long**.

Mostly eat fish but also squid, seals, sea lions and even the occasional **marine iguana**.

Are often confused with **dusky** sharks.

CHAPTER 4

Chickened Out

Mum and Dad snorkelled off towards the shore.

I had told them I'd come later, and made up some excuse about still being hungry. I walked into the miniature boat kitchen and opened the fridge. It was full of jars and bottles. But they weren't filled with jams and pickles, like most normal people's fridges. Our fridge was always filled with fish guts and other weird stuff.

I picked up a jar labelled *Specimen B*. Half a jellyfish blobbed around inside it. Its see-through tentacles were like long, floating strings of snot. "Bleurgh," I said, putting it back. Three bumpy sea cucumbers sat on the shelf above. They were stiff and shrivelled now. "Yuck!"

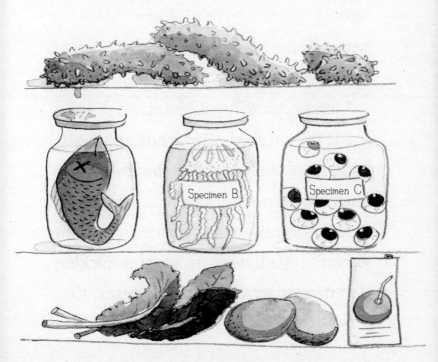

They reminded me of the disgusting ox tongue Pops once cooked up for lunch. There was no way I was going to eat that, either.

As I closed the fridge door, I heard someone behind me.

"Bwok bok bok." I turned to see Emely sitting on the bench, laughing.

"Shut up," I snapped. Why was she calling ME a chicken? I'd never seen her get in the water.

"No need to be nasty," she said.

"Me? Nasty? What about YOU?"

"Chill out, I was just having fun with you. Here, I'll make you something to eat," said Emely.

"No thanks, I'm not hungry any more," I said, walking back out to the deck. I really didn't get that girl.

I flopped backwards onto the couch. I was still wearing my smelly wetsuit. It was so boring being stuck on a boat in a faraway place. I wished I could hang out with my schoolmates, but that was impossible ... they were on the other side of the world.

Mum and Dad pulled me out too, so I didn't even go to a normal school any more. Now all my lessons were done online.

I grabbed my laptop, hoping there was a message from one of my friends.

Nope, nothing.

Then the internet connection dropped out. I sighed, and looked at the "school" file on my desktop. I figured I should probably find out what my first assignment was.

Click.

TEACHER: MRS SNOOGLE

ASSIGNMENT 1a: SEA CREATURES

"Great," I moaned, and snapped my laptop shut.

"Well, that should be easy for you," said a voice from behind me.

I jumped. I hadn't heard her sneak up. "Here you go," said Emely, handing me a glass of green slush.

"Ummm, what is that?" I asked.

"It's a smoothie ... for you."

"I'm not thirsty, thanks," I said, wondering why she was suddenly being nice to me.

"Why are you being nice to me?" I asked.

"This is my way of saying sorry for pranking you. Plus, I'm really good at inventing smoothie flavours."

"What *was* with the pranks?" I asked.

She shrugged. "Just bored, I guess. Anyway, if you don't want this, I'll have it." Emely plonked a straw in the smoothie and sulked off.

"Wait!" I called. "Okay, I'll try it."

Maybe she was all right. If anyone knew what it was like to be bored on a boat, it was me.

I took the smoothie. "What's in it?" I asked, smelling the thick green liquid like a sniffer dog.

"Coconut, mango, kale and some other vegetables."

The smoothie *did* smell like mango.

"No seawater?" I asked.

"No seawater – cross my heart and hope to die," she said, then licked her finger and left.

"Thanks," I said.

Green smoothies were my favourite. Mum makes one she calls a Shrek smoothie. This one looked similar, but it was more of an army-green than a Shrek-green.

I gave it one last sniff before taking a little sip.

CHAPTER 5

Sick Burps

It wasn't bad.

I had been worried, for a second, that

the smoothie was another prank.

It was delicious. Not salty at all.

Gulp, gulp, gulp...

BURP!

"Pardon me," I said, looking around.
But no one was there to hear me belch –
which was a waste, really. It was a ripper!

BURRRP!

"Whoa," I said, thumping my chest with my fist. Then up came another ... BURRRP! Then another ... BURRRP!

BURP, BURP, BURRRRRP!

Wow, they were some sick burps, I thought. Suddenly my body felt all tingly. My stomach twisted. I bent over, my elbows on my knees.

The boat seemed to be spinning ... faster and faster, around and around. Everything went green and fuzzy. Droplets of sweat ran down my face, dripped onto my wetsuit and bounced off in slow motion. *I must be overheating in this thing,* I thought. But before I could get the sweaty wettie off, my stomach knotted.

Sick bubbles began shooting up the back of my throat. I stumbled to the side of the boat, but my feet were going in the opposite direction to my head. It was like trying to run right after a dizzy-whizzy.

"BLUURGHH!"

Green smoothie exploded out of my mouth, down the side of the boat and into the ocean.

"BLAAAGHH!"

More vomit flowed like water from a burst fire hydrant.

"Are you okay?" I heard Emely call.

"Nooo," I groaned. "What was in that smoothie?"

"Just fruit and vegetables!" she said.

"WHAT fruit and vegetables?" I asked.

"Mango, coconut ... and a teensy bit of ... ah, cucumber," she said.

"SEA CU – BURP – CUMBER?" I yelled.

"Yes," she squeaked. "I'm sorry. I didn't mean for..."

I vomited again, my nostrils streaming green smoothie.

"Aaaand ... jellyfish," Emely said, covering her mouth.

"**Ooooorrrgh!** You've poisoned me!"

"Here, have some water!" said Emely, handing me a bottle.

As I reached for the water, everything started to turn black.

"I think ... I'm ... going to ... pass..."

JELLYFISH

Have no **brains**, **bones** or **hearts**.

Can **clone** themselves.

When grouped together are called a "**smack**" or "**bloom**" or "**swarm**".

Can glow in the dark. Some species are **bioluminescent**, creating their own light.

The largest is the **lion's mane jellyfish**, which can grow longer than a **blue whale**.

CHAPTER 6

Monster Headache

"Ooooow."

My head was thumping. Waves were lapping at my toes.

I had to squint as everything was way too bright.

"Ooohhh," I moaned, sand crunching between my teeth. I could feel my snorkel pressing into my neck. I tried to lift my face out of the sand, but it felt

like a tractor was parked on my head.
As I tried again, a big black tail flopped
onto my face. "AAAHHHH!" I screamed,
scrambling up onto my knees.

A huge ugly reptile rolled off my back.
I scuttled across the sand like a crazy crab.
What was that monster? As my fumbling
legs tried to run, I looked back at it.

DONK!

I hit a wall of black volcanic rock.
I dropped to the sand, stunned.

"WHAT WAS THAT THING?" I gasped, trying to catch my breath.

"And WHERE AM I?" I added, spinning around on the spot.

I didn't recognise the place. It was a much smaller island than where we'd been anchored before. Bright white sand, black rocks, a few bushes and ... nothing!

Except ocean.

There was ocean everywhere.

"Wait ... the boat."

I ran into the water. My eyeballs bounced from side to side like a tennis ball.

I couldn't see the boat.

CHAPTER 7

Coma-nosed

Staring out towards the horizon, all I could see was blue. I rubbed my eyes and looked again. The blanket of blue ocean stretched out to meet a wall of hazy blue sky. Only a few black bumps of island broke the never-ending blue. I felt so small. I wondered if this minuscule island was even visible on Google Earth. I squinted and searched the ocean even harder for our boat.

There was no big white boat. Not even a small speck of a boat. It was gone.

My parents were gone!

"HELP!" I yelled. "MUM? DAD?"

Nothing.

"HELLLLLLLLP!"

Still nothing.

I stood in the shallow water, staring at the ocean like a zombie. *I must be dreaming,* I thought.

I watched a small jellyfish float by. It looked just like the one in the fridge.

"JELLYFISH!" I cried, as I suddenly remembered Emely's jellyfish and sea cucumber smoothie.

"EMELY!" I roared.

That deadly green concoction must have put me in a coma! *This must all be a crazy dream*, I thought. *Yes, that's it, it's just a dream.* I closed my eyes and breathed deeply, slowly.

In ... and out.

I just had to work out how to wake myself up – then everything would be okay.

I looked around for something, anything.

The ocean!

SPLASH!

Dunking my head in the sea didn't do the trick.

"OUCH!"

Neither did slapping myself in the face.

How else do you wake yourself from a nightmare?

I pinched my ear as hard as I could. I felt it, but it wasn't enough to wake me up.

A red crab scuttled over a nearby rock. *Ah-ha, that might work*, I thought. I knelt down and crept as close as I could. I stuck out my nose, closed my eyes and waited. Surely it wouldn't actually hurt ... this was just a dream, right?

But nothing happened. Again, I nudged forwards, closer and closer to the crab, till the tip of my nose bumped its claw.

NIP!

"YEOOOOOWWW!"

The crab hung off my nostril. I stamped my feet up and down, screaming. Its claw tightened, pinching even harder. Tears sprung from my eyes. "Get off, get off!" I wailed, running up the beach and flapping my arms like a headless seagull. The pain was a hundred times worse than a stinger.

The cranky crustacean had almost ripped my nostril off when suddenly, I froze.

Right at my feet sat the big reptile.

Its ugly, smashed-in face looked me up and down, then it slowly lifted one sharp, clawed foot.

I'm going to die, I'm going to die! I thought. I had never been so scared in all my life.

And I was pretty sure I was NOT in a

jellyfish dream. Not even a sea cucumber coma ... it was far worse than that. It was REALITY, and that meant I really was lost on a deserted island ... with a

nose-nipping crab

and a

prehistoric kid-eating lizard!

GALAPAGOS SALLY LIGHTFOOT CRABS

Are often **bright red**, standing out against black volcanic rocks.

Begin life dark brown, becoming **brighter** and **brighter** every time they **moult**.

Enjoy eating **parasites** off marine iguanas.

Are **super-fast** and so **agile** they appear to walk on water.

CHAPTER 8

Lizard Ninja

I'd never seen anything like it. Except maybe in movies. It looked like a goanna, only its head was hard and spiky. It was like a miniature dragon.

"SHOO!" I squealed, the crab still hanging from my nose.

The lizard didn't budge.

"Go on, GET!" I said, stomping my foot. The angry crab swung from side to side. It was not letting go.

The lizard stared at me.

"RAAAHH! LEAVE ME ALONE!" I yelled, and kicked sand in its face. It leaped up and wrapped its front claws around the inside of my leg. My eyes bulged. Its back claws gripped my ankle as the four-legged monster climbed me like a coconut tree. I could feel the tips of its sharp claws pierce my wetsuit.

My mouth opened to scream, but nothing came out. The terrifying creature climbed higher and higher, then gripped my shoulder. Its long, spiky tail hung down my back like a punk-rocker's ponytail.

I was too scared to move.

Too scared to breathe...

BANG!

With one swipe the lizard karate chopped the crab right off my nose! The crustacean frisbeed through the air and plopped into the ocean. I stood, frozen, the lizard ninja still clamped to my shoulder.

Moving only my eyes, I looked at the creature. It had a head like a cactus. Its face was covered in bumps and barnacles.

Definitely a dragon. Or maybe some type of mutant ninja creature? I wished Dad was with me. I bet he'd know what it was. He'd certainly know whether it ate kids or not.

Slowly bending my knees, I dropped to the sand. The lizard held on. Kneeling, I began to slowly walk my shaking arms forwards until I was lying flat on my stomach. The lizard's body now stretched down my back and along my leg. I waited for it to climb off, but it didn't move.

The reptile's head was so close to mine I could smell its stinky breath. At least I still had a nose, I guess. I squeezed my eyes shut and gave my shoulder a quick jolt. The lizard dug in its claws. Lucky I had my wetsuit on, or I'd be pricked all over like a sausage.

The creature wouldn't budge. I was too frightened to poke it – especially after seeing its mad ninja skills.

What could I do? I couldn't get the freaky lizard off. I was stuck. So I just had to lie there.

And lie there...

And lie there some more.

Would you like to know the thoughts you have when you're stuck on a deserted island with a lizard ninja on your back? Here's a sample:

Oh, no, I'm stuck on a deserted island with a lizard ninja on my back!

How did this happen?

Where are my parents?

Why haven't they found me yet?

My tummy hurts.

I lay there, watching my tears sink into the sand.

"Hey," a voice said.

Huh? Did the lizard just talk? Now I really was going mad.

"Ummm ... did you just talk?" I whispered back.

"Yes!" said the voice.

"Holy cow!" I cried. "It talks! It talks!"

"Oh wow," said the voice, "you've really lost the plot... What are you doing to that iguana?"

Fish Kid Facts

MARINE IGUANAS

Sneeze **salt boogers** from salt-excreting glands in their nostrils.

Favourite food is **green algae**.

Are the world's only lizards that **forage and feed** in the sea.

Are only found in the **Galapagos Islands**.

Chapter 9
Cold-blooded

"Emely! Is it really you?" I asked, still facedown in the sand.

I was so relieved to hear her voice. Well, kind of. I was still dirty about the smoothie.

"Where are we? Where are Mum and Dad? Where's the boat?"

"It's just us. And thanks to you, we've lost the boat!" she said.

"Me?"

"Yes, you. The last thing I remember is you grabbing on to me. You took us overboard! Now we're STUCK HERE with no boat!"she yelled.

"Shhh, can't you see this lizard is about to eat me?" I whispered. "And you seem to have forgotten that it was *you* who poisoned *me*!"

"People eat raw seafood all the time. It's not my fault you're allergic. Now get out from under that marine iguana."

"Marine iguana?" I asked.

"Yeah, they're harmless," said Emely.

I didn't believe for one second it was harmless. It was the most beastly looking thing I'd ever seen.

"It's trying to roast me in this wetsuit. I'll be done by dinner time," I said, still too terrified to move.

"It thinks you're a rock."

"Huh?"

"You're covered in black, just like those," she said, pointing to the black rocks all around us.

"Oh!" I suddenly realised why he was glued to me. He was trying to get warm! He was a cold-blooded lizard, and my wetsuit was now hotter than a barbecue on Australia Day.

"I'll dunk us in the sea, that'll get him off."

"Just flick it off," said Emely.

The creature's claws were as long and sharp as knives. There was no way I was going to flick any part of it.

I rolled slowly onto my side. The iguana climbed around me until he was on top again.

I rolled further, right onto my back. He clawed his way up onto my front. We were now face to face. Pushing my tummy and the iguana up, I started shuffling along on my hands and feet. The lizard stared at me as I crab-walked us towards the ocean.

"If only I had a camera," said Emely. "You look ridiculous."

In we went. A wave lapped over my stomach and his toes. As I inched deeper, the iguana stood up. Water washed beneath him.

I shuffled deeper again, enough to sink completely in. The lizard floated off me.

"It worked!" I called out to Emely. She shook her head at me.

But the lizard didn't scramble to shore like I thought he would. He actually seemed quite happy floating in the water. He flicked his tail from side to side as he swam circles around me.

"It can swim!" I said.

"MARINE...IGUANA," said Emely, as if she was talking to a two-year-old. "You know – 'swimming lizard'?"

The marine iguana ducked his head and dived below the surface.

How had I not heard of a marine iguana before? I pulled my mask over my eyes and stuck my head under for another look. My cut nose stung in the salt water.

The iguana wiggled his body, gliding through the water. He swam like a giant tadpole with his legs dragging behind, his long tail acting like a propeller.

He swam deeper, then looped back around, bobbing up next to me again.

"Stop playing about," called Emely, from the shore.

The marine iguana dived below again. I followed him under. I spat out my snorkel as it filled with water. We swam away from the shore, deeper and deeper, until both our tummies were resting on the sandy bottom. The iguana wiggled closer until we were nose to snout. He stared into my eyes, and I felt a strange cold pulse fill my chest, then radiate all the way out to my fingertips. The marine iguana held my gaze.

Was this some kind of spell? What did he want with me?

Suddenly I realised I hadn't been up for air in a while. My body didn't feel the need to breathe, but my head panicked. My legs kicked furiously till I broke the surface, bursting through.

"Whoa!" I yelled after taking a big breath. I looked to the shore, but Emely wasn't there. She was frantically swimming towards me. It was like she was going for gold at the Olympics, or had a great white clipping her toenails.

"You idiot!" she yelled. "I thought you had drowned!" Emely pushed down on my shoulders, like she WAS actually trying to drown me.

"Did you see that?" I asked. "That was sick! I was under for ages."

"What were you doing?" Emely asked.

"I just forgot to breathe."

"What do you mean, you 'forgot'? People don't just forget to breathe!"

I tried again. The marine iguana was still under water, so I dived down to meet him. This time I didn't panic. The chill filled my chest and trickled down to my toes. Time stopped as we washed back and forth over the rippled seabed. Emely dived down too. Five times she tried holding her breath, but she couldn't last more than a minute. I stayed under the whole time.

"That was insane!" she said when I finally came back up. "How did you...?"

"Pretty cool, huh?" I pulled up my mask.

"Something fishy is going on," said Emely.

The iguana popped up between us, and coughed green goo onto my wetsuit.

"GREEN SMOOTHIE!" we shouted.

CHAPTER 10
Fish Kid

That fishy stuff wasn't poisonous ... it was powerful!

"Do you think it was the sea cucumber?" asked Emely, treading water.

"Well, Dad *did* say something about it having healing powers. What else was in that smoothie?"

"Could have been the jellyfish?"

"Or a chemical reaction between

them both," I said.

The smoothie had somehow mutated me. I could dive for ages, without even needing a scuba tank.

Wow, I thought, *how much will Dad love this? And Pops, too. I could rescue all his snagged fishhooks.*

"It's like you have a real superpower," said Emely. "A fish superpower!"

"It *is* pretty awesome," I said, wondering if there was anything else I could do. As the marine iguana swam towards the shore, I realised he must have known somehow. Had he been trying to tell me all along?

"Race you!" called Emely, swimming after the lizard. I swam as fast as I could … which turned out to be pretty freaking fast! I mean, not like the speed of light or anything, but faster than any other kid could swim. I zipped past Emely and the marine iguana.

"What the—" said Emely.

"How fast was that!" I said, shaking my head dry.

As Emely stood in the shallows, I tested my skills again.

ZOOM!

Another super-speedy loop of the bay.

"FISH KID!" yelled Emely, punching the air. "Move over Spider-Man, it's ...

Emely grabbed my shoulders and shook me. Her face lit up.

"Do you see how amazing this is?" she said, looking like she was about to burst. "You could save people with powers like these. Maybe you'll save the world one day!" Emely was even more excited than I was – if that was possible.

"I'll have to start wearing my undies on the outside of my wetsuit!" I joked. Emely fell on the beach laughing.

"And HE will be your sidekick!" she said, pointing to the marine iguana.

"Yes!" I said with a clap.

We tried to think of a super sidekick name for him.

Lizonardo

Fish Kid Junior

Splash

(because it rhymes with Flash)

Banana

(because it rhymes with iguana)

Wolvermarine

(because of his claws)

Reptilian

None were any good. Except maybe Wolvermarine. That one was my idea.

I patted his ugly, bumpy head again. "What about Handsome?" I said, as a joke.

"Haha. Or Guapo!" said Emely. "It means 'handsome' in Spanish."

It actually sounded pretty cool. All the locals spoke Spanish, and the lizard was a local after all.

"Guapo it is," I said. "The one and only Lizard Ninja!"

His new name suited him. I sat down

next to Guapo and stared out to sea. That's when my super-bubble burst. I wondered where Mum and Dad and the skipper could be. Why hadn't they found us yet?

"I hope these powers can save US somehow," I said.

Emily sat down as well. "I hope so too."

Neither of us said anything more after that.

I'd have given all my powers back just to see my parents again.

CHAPTER 11

Seven. Old. Sea lions.

There was nothing on the island but sand, black volcanic rock and spiky cactus trees. From the top of the tiny island we could see ocean all around. Although there were a few bumps on the horizon, there was no sign of our boat. No sign of ANY boat.

I looked down at the SOS signal I had drawn on the beach. Pops had taught me that SOS meant "help".

"Suck On Squids?" said Emely. "Or Stinky Orange Socks?"

It actually stood for Save Our Souls, and she already knew that. She had lived on boats most of her life.

"Do you think anyone will see it?" asked Emely. She had a point. From up here, my SOS signal looked Small Or Stupid!

I could see Guapo clearly, though. His little dark body stood out on the white sand. There were seven other big blobs on the beach, too.

"Is SOS still spelled SOS in Spanish?" I asked Emely.

"I think so," said Emely. "It's Morse code... Wait, what's that?" she said, shushing me.

Wck-wck-wck...

I stood still and listened.

Wucka-wucka-wucka...

"It's a chopper!" I said, searching the sky.

"THERE!" said Emely, pointing to a little dot just below the clouds.

"HEY! HEY! OVER HERE!" I called, flapping my arms about. Finally, we were going to be saved!

As the helicopter came closer, we jumped up and down, waving our arms like crazy.

"OVER HERE! OVER HERE!" we screamed.

WUCKA-WUCKA-WUCKA!

The helicopter flew right towards us ...

... then straight over.

"Did they see us?" asked Emely, puffing.

"I don't know," I replied. I worried they might have missed us. Especially me in my wetsuit. I was camouflaged against the black rocks.

"The beach!" I said. "We'll stand out much better on the sand."

We raced back down the hill. As we ran, I stubbed my toe on a log of driftwood. I stumbled, but Emely was going too fast to stop. She bowled me over. Arms and legs tangled and tumbled as we avalanched onto the beach.

After a messy crashlanding I ran back up to fetch the driftwood.

I dug it into the sand, carving a huge arc.

Guapo watched as Emely dug out the last "S". Then he stood up, snorted and strutted past us. His tail snaked along behind him as he headed up the beach.

"Oh, thanks for your help!" I yelled as I spun in a circle to make a bigger "O".

Guapo went off towards the sea lions lazing on the beach. Next thing, I saw him headbutt one! What a crazy lizard. I kept working on my letter "O". The sea lions started stirring and grunting. Then the stupid lizard bonked his head on another!

"SHHH!" I said, trying to listen out for the helicopter. I hoped it would come back soon. It HAD to.

Just as we finished our SOS signal, the sea lions began honking and hobbling along the beach. "SHOO!"

I yelled. Guapo kept chasing them, nipping at their flippers. They were huge, and they were headed straight for us. We bolted up the hill. When we reached the top, I looked down at our signal. The sea lions were smudging it as they dragged their fat bellies across the letters.

Wucka-wucka-wucka.

"The helicopter!" called Emely.

"SHOO! SHOO!" I flapped and yelled as Guapo kept herding the sea lions.

WUCKA-WUCKA-WUCKA

"HELP, HELP!" we screamed and waved. "OVER HERE!"

The helicopter flew over again, but further out this time. My arms dropped. I was sure it hadn't seen us. Emely sank to her knees. The helicopter was gone.

I could tell Emely was gutted, but I was FURIOUS, and ready to barbecue Guapo! Just as I was about to march back down the beach, Emely grabbed my leg.

"Look," she said, pointing.

I looked at the sea lions. I couldn't believe my eyes...

Seven. Old. Sea lions. Just as Guapo had arranged them.

Fish Kid Facts

GALAPAGOS SEA LIONS

Are the largest **endemic land animal** in the Galapagos Islands.

Are "pinnipeds", which means they are **fin-footed**, like seals and walruses.

Have **ear flaps**, which is how you can tell sea lions apart from seals.

In Spanish are called *lobos marinos* or **sea wolves**.

CHAPTER 12

Food Fight

The SOS of sea lions slept on the beach all afternoon. But the helicopter didn't come back. As we watched the sun sink, I wondered if Mum and Dad had been inside it. They had to be searching for us.

Guapo crawled up and sat on my leg. He let me run a finger over his hard, bumpy head. "Guapo the Lizard Ninja," I said, beginning to stroke his tough neck. He pushed against my hand the way a dog leans into a good scratch. What a trusty sidekick he was turning out to be. Karate chopping killer crabs, sea lion SOS signals ... and I would never have discovered my fish powers if it wasn't for him either.

"So what's for dinner, chef?" I asked.

Guapo snorted. A white salty booger splattered on my face. Emely lost it, cracking up.

"Gross!" I said, spitting out the crusty bits. "EEEUWW! I prefer burgers to boogers, thanks!"

Guapo slid off my leg and headed for the water. Off for a meal of seaweed, I guessed.

"There is nothing on this island," said Emely. "No berries, no bird eggs and definitely no burgers!"

"There was a crab," I said. "But I'm not trying another one of your seafood experiments."

"Hey, Fish Kid, you could catch us a fish!" said Emely. "You can swim like a fish and stay under forever ... so surely you can hunt like a fish?"

Was she right? Could I catch us a fish? It was worth a try.

As I waded into the water, I looked out for Guapo. He was gone. Were the powers even still with me? Would they work without him? Maybe he was the super one, not me.

A school of baitfish swam by. They hovered in the shallows. I bobbed under and waited. Three dinner-sized fish swam through, breaking up the tiny fish cloud.

Okay, Fish Kid, I said to myself. *Let's do this.*

I kept still, waiting for my moment. I felt the cold rush in my lungs. I didn't panic. That's when I knew I could stay under – the power was working.

The three fish circled past again.

Ready ... set ... GO!

I launched through the water and my hand shot out. I missed!

Kick, chase, dart. It felt like slow motion, but it happened so fast.

The fish split up. I chased one, grabbed it...

GOT IT!

I gripped it with both hands and tried to hold on. It wiggled and squirmed, fighting my grasp.

I burst to the surface.

"I got one, I got one!" I yelled. Emely jumped up, her mouth hanging open in shock. I couldn't believe I'd caught one either. And with my bare hands, too. Or should I say BEAR hands. RRAAA!

The slippery fish jerked like crazy.

"What now?" I yelled.

Emely ran into the water.

"It's too slippery!" I called, trying to hold on as it almost flipped free.

"Bite it!" said Emely.

"Huh?"

"Bite it. KILL IT!" she screamed.

I really didn't want to bite the flipping fish, but I didn't want to lose our dinner either.

My head wiggled, mouth open, trying to line up a bite.

"Do it, QUICK!" yelled Emely.

CHOMP!

I bit the fish on the back. Its head stuck out one side of my mouth, and the tip of its tail kept stabbing me in the eye. Its scales were hard, like metal.

My teeth didn't make a dent. The fish gave another flick, and a spike pierced my tongue.

"AAAARGHH!" I yelped.

As I opened my mouth, the fish leaped out. It flopped back into the ocean and swam away.

"Owwww," I said, holding my sore, scaly tongue.

"Nooo!" cried Emely. "You let it go!"

CHAPTER 13

Night Terror

Guapo, Emely and I sat on the sand, watching the ocean swallow the sun. We were tired, cold, hungry and scared.

"What a crazy day," said Emely.

"The craziest day in the history of crazy," I agreed.

It was getting dark – far too dark for helicopter searches. We were stuck there for the night.

"They should have found us by now," said Emely.

"I know," I replied. "Do you think I'll have to swim for it tomorrow?"

We both knew my fish powers were our only hope. There was no way Emely could swim that far – no normal human could. The thought of swimming out through the deep terrified me. Maybe it was safer to stay on the island. But we wouldn't last long without food.

My tummy rumbled.

"If you do, I'm coming with you," said Emely. "I'll hold on to your shoulders."

"Ummm ... I guess that could work," I said.

Mum's shark photo flashed into my mind. I shuddered.

"Why are you so scared of the ocean?"

asked Emely, as if reading my mind.

"Sea creatures," I said.

"Sea creatures? But your parents love them. They swim with them all the time."

"That makes it worse!" I said. "Giant squid, sea snakes, viperfish, MEGAMOUTH SHARKS! Most kids don't even know they exist."

"Well, marine iguanas are sea creatures ... and look at you two now."

Guapo was stretched out on top of me, snorting and snoring. Every now and again he'd dig his claws into my butt. *Must be having ninja dreams,* I thought. But I didn't mind. I wanted him close by.

"Strange that it's just him, though," said Emely.

"What do you mean?" I asked.

"Marine iguanas are everywhere around here. There are usually hundreds of them crawling all over each other. It's weird to see just one," she said.

As it got darker, I noticed a glow out at sea.

"I think I see lights. Maybe it's a town? Or a ship?" I said, pointing.

Emely was now curled up tightly like a sea snail. She must have been cold without a wetsuit. She lifted her head to take a look.

"Could be. Or a volcano," she said, squinting.

As the darkness grew, so did my imagination. Every little noise became a skyscraping monster. There was no way I was going to sleep.

"I wish my parents were here," I said. Emely didn't reply. Was she asleep?

Something rustled in the bushes. I stayed dead still, desperately wanting my mum and dad. They wouldn't have been scared. Dad would be studying the creature in the bushes. Mum would snuggle with me and keep me warm. We'd stare at the glow on the ocean, telling each other dragon stories. Mum and Dad would probably love it.

But they weren't with me. And I knew they wouldn't be sleeping either. They'd be staring out at the same dark sea, thinking the same thing I was:

Will I ever see them again?

CHAPTER 14

Goodbye Guapo

Faster than a speeding mullet ... stronger than a bull shark ... it's Fish Kid!

Well, the speedy bit was true.

Emely was waiting, standing knee-deep in the water.

"It's now or never, Fish Kid," she called.

I checked the beach for Guapo, but he wasn't there.

"I'm not sure we should do this," I said.

GRrrrrrr went my stomach for the billionth time. It was emptier than a dog's bowl after dinner.

"Have you seen Guapo?" I asked Emely.

"Nope. He's probably off feeding. Let's go!"

"Wait there," I said, running up the beach. I climbed to the top of the island. Still no Guapo.

The sky was grey and cloudy. It was difficult to see the islands in the distance, but one chunk of land seemed closer than the others. It was in the same direction as the glow I'd seen last night. I figured that bump in the blue was going to be our best bet.

Could Fish Kid really swim THAT far? There was only one way to find out.

I bounded back down to the beach. "Goodbye, stinky sea lions." I checked the rocks one last time, but Guapo was nowhere to be seen.

"GOODBYE, GUAPOOO," I called, sad that I couldn't give him one last scaly scratch. It was probably a good thing, I decided. It would have been hard to say goodbye.

I waded into the water. Emely stood behind me and put her hands on my shoulders. We walked out a little further, then I plonked us in. Cold water flooded my wetsuit. Poor Emely only had the shorts and T-shirt she'd been wearing when she fell overboard.

She held on as I started to swim.

"Giddy-up," she said. But when I tried to power off, I sank. Every couple of strokes we'd go under again.

"Please don't drown me," said Emely, spluttering.

Grrrrrrr. My stomach growled again. I bet Superman never had to fly on an empty stomach.

"I'll try just kicking," I said. With both arms stretched out in front, I tried smaller kicks this time. Slow at first, then faster, faster. We were off!

My legs were strong, like a motor. I felt like I could swim a marathon. Emely gripped my shoulders tight, as fish and turtles blurred by. I was having so much fun, I forgot all about scary sea creatures.

Before long, the sandy sea floor dropped off and the ocean became deep and dark. Emely spotted some rocks poking out of the water ahead, so I slowed us down a little. A school of huge fish, almost bigger than us, swam past. The water was murky and speckled.

Some long, pointy fish swam our way. They looked kind of snaky. As they got closer, one opened its mouth, showing us its razor teeth.

"Barracuda!" I whispered. I felt Emely grip me tighter as we sped around them.

"Savage-looking things," she said, wiping her eyes.

As I swam closer to the rocks I spotted a dolphin a few metres below the surface. Or was it a sea lion?

A ribbon of silver fish streamed by.

Splash! Something whooshed past my face.

"What was that?" I gasped.

It grazed my foot as it looped around us. I felt a sharp prick as something pierced through the arm of my wetsuit. I'd felt that before.

"GUAPO?" I said.

The dolphin shape now looked bigger. Guapo rammed his skull into my head, then scrambled up onto a rock. "Hey!" I yelled.

Emely climbed onto the rock after Guapo, but there wasn't enough room for me. Guapo dived into the water and plunged straight down.

"Wait here," I said to Emely. "I think he wants me to follow."

I took a breath and dived down. Deeper and deeper we went. Guapo squeezed into a hole in the reef, so I did the same, and held on just as he did. As I felt the fish power fill my lungs, the big shape passed over us. From below it looked completely black.

It was shaped like a capital "T".

Even in murky water, it was suddenly
very clear what it was ...
A HAMMERHEAD SHARK!
"FAR OUT!" I yelled silently.
Then another one swam past ...
and another.

Fish Kid Facts

BARRACUDA

Have strong jaws and two rows of **razor-sharp** teeth.

With one bite, can **chop** a fish right in half.

Are **speedy hunters**, sometimes swimming in bursts of speed over 25 mph.

Like **shiny things**, so don't wear silver jewellery or watches when diving with them.

CHAPTER 15

Shivers!

Twenty-two hammerhead sharks glided over our heads. The blue glow of the ocean made it look like they were flying in the sky, like fighter jets in formation.

Mum once told me a group of sharks was called a shiver of sharks. Now I knew why. They should have been called a poo-your-pants of sharks!

But the more we watched, the less

I shivered. It was kind of mesmerising being that deep. It felt like someone had shrunk me down and plonked me into an aquarium.

I wished I had a camera. My mates would never believe this.

Guapo and I held tight. We watched the sharks circle the tower of reef that led up to Emely, who was still standing on the very peak.

Don't jump in, I urged, wishing she could hear my thoughts.

The sharks cruised by once more, then vanished into the blue, like starships.

I gave Guapo two thumbs up. He had protected me again. He sure was some sidekick. I was beginning to think he was actually the super one, not me.

"Hey, you two, what's going on?"

asked Emely as we popped back up.

"Hammerhead sharks! Twenty-two of them – you should have seen them! They were like fighter jets, they cruised right over our heads! And Guapo and I..."

"Whoa, slow down, Fish Kid. You're starting to sound like your parents," said Emely, smirking.

It was true, I was buzzing. I couldn't believe I'd just had my first shark encounter. I still thought they were scary, but awesome, too.

I eventually convinced Emely that the sharks were gone. She climbed down from the rock and onto my back, and we swam off. This time Guapo led the way.

From then on, I constantly checked in all directions for sharky shapes.

After a while Guapo slowed down,

then stopped. We bobbed in the rolling waves, trying to look about. Emely had goosebumps all over her.

"TOWN AHOY!" she announced.

I could see tiny white specks that had to be boats and houses.

"WOOHOO!" yelled Emely, slapping the water. "Let's go, let's go!"

"Hold on tight," I called as we powered off towards the distant town. Strangely, even after all that swimming, I didn't feel tired. I'd soon see my parents, and the skipper. I thought about how relieved they'd be. They were going to love Guapo.

"Guapo!" I said, spinning around. We couldn't see him anywhere.

"Where is he?" I asked. But Emely had no idea either. We swam back until

I spotted a little black blob. He was swimming so slowly.

"There you are," I said. Guapo seemed a bit stiff.

"He's tired," said Emely. "We've come a long way."

Guapo stopped moving completely.

"Come on buddy, not far now," I said. But I knew we were still a long way off. He stared at me with half-closed eyes, his legs and tail hanging down.

I could tell he was done.

Fish Kid Facts

HAMMERHEAD SHARKS

Can see **360** degrees.

Have flat, **hammer-shaped** heads that help to pin down **stingrays**, their favourite meal.

Have special sensory cells that detect **electrical fields** given off by hidden prey.

Have ten different species – the **largest** is the Great Hammerhead Shark.

CHAPTER 16

A Boat!

I placed my hand under Guapo's belly and lifted his cold body to the surface.

"He's freezing," I said.

Guapo had been in the water far too long. He needed a hot black rock to lie on. But there were no rocks in sight. And hardly any sun poking out through the clouds.

"I'll carry him," said Emely, scooping

him under one arm. "I can still hold on."

Emely wedged her spare hand into the neckhole of my wetsuit. It was tricky balancing both Emely and Guapo on my back, and we swam much more slowly. Wave after wave smashed us in the face.

"Stop," said Emely, struggling to hold on. "He's not doing too well."

Guapo's eyes were now completely closed.

"Wake up, buddy," I said, rubbing his head.

Nothing.

He didn't move or blink or anything.

"We have to get help," I said.

Emely tried to tuck Guapo back under her arm.

"Shhh," I said. I thought I'd heard something.

Prrrrrrrtt ptt ptt ptt.

"A motor!" We both put our ears to the water.

"Sounds like a lawnmower," said Emely. "Could it be a boat?" I hoped it was a rescue boat, but any boat would do.

"Guapo! We're going to be saved," I said.

I swam us towards the noise.

"There!" shouted Emely.

An old wooden boat was bobbing on the spot. I rushed over and we yelled, but no one answered.

"Hello? Anyone?" called Emely. "They can't hear us over

that racket," she said, letting go of my shoulder.

I climbed the rusty ladder at the back of the boat. Emely passed Guapo up, then climbed aboard too.

We looked at the rusty hunk of motor on the back deck. Tubes fed down into the sea.

"What's it for?" I asked. "Looks like it's made from old washing machine parts."

The motor putted and spluttered.

"I've seen something like this before," said Emely. "It's for air. Like scuba air – but a hose instead of a tank. Someone must be out diving."

"Looks pretty dodgy," I said.

I laid Guapo carefully on the warm wooden deck. He slowly stretched out to soak up the warmth, still keeping his eyes closed.

"Hello?" I called again. There didn't seem to be anyone about at all.

"Check upstairs," said Emely.

As I was about to climb the cockpit ladder, I noticed two big metal tubs. They looked like old fishing eskies. I lifted the lid of one.

"Whoa! Take a look at this," I said. Emely rushed over. The tub was filled with hundreds of sea cucumbers.

"Poachers!" we both whispered.

I opened the second tub. More sea cucumbers. They looked just like the specimens Dad had collected. We had to get off the boat – fast. Just as we were about to bail, I stopped.

"A superhero would save the sea cucumbers," I said.

"No way!" said Emely. "What if the poacher comes back?"

I didn't want to risk Emely's life, or mine, but part of me felt it was now my job to save the sea cucumbers.

"I have to try! You keep watch," I said, pushing the tub as hard as I could. It was way too heavy to shift. Emely huffed, then tried to help, yet the tub wouldn't budge.

"Shame you don't have the strength of a whale," she said.

We began throwing them one by one into the sea. But that was going to take far too long. Emely rummaged through the rusty cupboards and found a small bucket.

"Here," she said, chucking it to me. As Emely kept searching the boat, I bailed bucket after bucket of seawater out of the tub. Then I tried pushing it again, this time tipping the tub on to its side. Water and sea cucumbers spilled out across the deck. Some rolled over poor Guapo. I shoved the sea cucumbers back in the tub. Without all the water, I could finally move it.

"Yes!" I said, pushing the tub to the edge, where I tipped out the lot. Sea cucumbers rolled and plopped back into the ocean.

A stream of bubbles erupted from the sea before I could bail out the second tub.

"The diver!" I whispered.

I yanked the zip on my wetsuit and picked up Guapo. He was cold and stiff, like a frozen pineapple. I stuffed him down the front of my wettie, his head just poking out. Arrrghhh! He was so spiky! It was like trying to smuggle an echidna in your pyjamas!

The man at the end of the tubes bobbed to the surface.

"Oi!" he shouted, about to climb the ladder.

"Emely, jump!" I dived right over his head. Emely leaped over the side. The poacher whacked his reg back in his mouth. As I hit the water, he grabbed my ankle. I kicked like crazy, trying to shake him off. I pulled and pulled at the water, swimming as hard as I could, and dodging falling sea cucumbers. But the man held on, yanking at my leg.

I kept trying to kick us further away from the boat. I knew he'd have to run out of hose at some point.

YANK! He finally let go.

"PHEW!"

The diver returned to the surface. My heart was pounding. Suddenly I thought of Emely. I burst up to see the poacher charging straight at her.

Emely was swimming like mad, but the poacher was wearing flippers, so he was faster. I chased hard. I had to beat him.

Guapo's spikes cut into me with every stroke.

Kick, kick, kick.

The poacher was close...

Kick, kick.

What would he do to her...

Kick...

"NO!" I yelled. "Leave her alone."

Emely stopped swimming. She turned to face him...

PSSSSSSSSHHHH!

A line of smoke shot between them and up into the sky. The flare burst bright like a firecracker. The poacher turned and bolted back to his boat. I caught up to Emely.

"Nice work," I said as she grabbed my shoulders. I swam like someone had lit a firecracker in my pants. I didn't look back.

Guapo's spikes still pressed into my chest. I hadn't felt him move at all. I tried to focus on swimming, but couldn't help wondering...

Was he even still alive?

CHAPTER 17

In Hot Water

Wucka–WUCKA–WUCKA.

A boat rushed towards us as the helicopter hovered above.

"They saw the flare!" said Emely.

"HERE! OVER HERE!" we shouted.

"BODHI! EMELY!" called Mum as the boat stopped. "Grab on!" She tossed the life ring, and Dad hurled himself into the water.

It was them! I couldn't believe it. They'd found us.

The skipper pulled Emely aboard.

"Bodhi! Bodhi!" Mum cried and waved from the boat. Dad swam up and squeezed the life out of me.

"Youch!" I yelped as Guapo's spikes stabbed my chest.

"You're alive!" said Dad, now examining my face with both hands. "What happened? Are you okay? We've been worried sick."

"Dad..."

"Bodhi, you're okay, aren't you?" Dad interrupted.

"Dad, you have to save him!" I begged. Finally Dad noticed Guapo's head poking out of my wetsuit.

"Let's get you both aboard," he said.

Emely was already wrapped in a blanket. The skipper reached out and pulled me up. Dad climbed up next. He lifted the lifeless lizard from my wetsuit, just before Mum netted me with a towel. She hugged me so tight I thought I'd pop. I hugged her harder.

"This is one cold marine iguana,"

said Dad. "Its limbs have completely seized up."

"His name is Guapo," I said, not wanting to let go of Mum. "You have to save him, Dad. Can you? Will he be all right?"

Dad didn't answer. He rushed off with Guapo in his arms.

I buried my head into Mum's warm hug.

"What happened?" asked the skipper. "Where on earth have you kids been?"

"First, they need food," said Mum, herding us into the kitchen.

The skipper jumped on the boat radio. He told the rescue station that Emely and I were aboard and safe.

They replied with more good news. The helicopter had spotted the poacher's boat. The water police soon caught him. They saw the tub of sea cucumbers and arrested him on the spot. So in the end it was a good thing I didn't tip them all out.

I was drooling like a bulldog as Mum pulled the snags out of the pan. Emely and I smashed a buttered bun each while we waited for the snags to cool down. Bread and butter had never tasted so good in all my life. I grabbed two hot dogs before Mum could get them onto the tray and went to find Dad. He had placed Guapo in a tub of warm water.

"We'll just have to wait and see," said Dad. "He has a lot of thawing out to do."

Dad told me that marine iguanas are ectothermic. "That means they can't internally regulate their body temperature like we can," he explained. But I already knew that. Guapo loved sitting on me to get warm.

Dad also said that, although they can hold their breath for up to an hour, marine iguanas usually only spend ten minutes in the water. Otherwise they get too cold – just like poor Guapo. We had been swimming for ages.

"We'll need to get him food," I said. "If he wakes up."

"Yes, that's a good idea," said Dad. As I stuffed mouthfuls of hot dog into my own gob, I told him that green weed was Guapo's favourite food. Dad said the green weed was called algae.

"I'll go for a dive to get some soon," he said.

"I'll come!" I said. Dad couldn't believe I wanted to get back in the water. He said he wasn't letting me off the boat again.

"But there's something I HAVE to show you," I begged. I couldn't wait to show Mum and Dad my fish powers. Just to see their faces. This was going to blow their socks AND their flippers off.

CHAPTER 18

The Examination

My parents got kitted up in all their dive gear, just as I'd asked them to. They were bobbing in the water, waiting.

"Don't forget your flippers, Bodhi," said Mum, adjusting her dive mask.

"Don't need them," I said.

Standing on the side of the boat, I took a deep breath – not that I was going to need it. I guess it was just habit.

I pointed my arms above my head, then dived over my parents and down into the ocean, swooping below them. I swirled around like a sea lion as they descended deeper. They both stared hard through their masks. I saw them look at each other, then back at me.

I dived further and waited for them again. Mum started waving and pointing up. I could see she was stressing. Dad came deeper till he was mask-to-mask with me. His frown relaxed a little as we swam along together. Mum was like a stunned mullet, her eyes wide open. I let out a burst of laughter. Dad pointed towards the surface. I wanted to stay longer, but I could tell they'd seen enough.

I kicked hard, shot past Mum and breached the surface.

"Bodhi! What on earth is going on?" said Dad when he finally popped up and pulled out his reg.

"Bodhi? You mean Fish Kid!" I said, laughing and punching one fist in the air.

"How did you do that? Is this some sort of trick? " asked Dad.

"Nope!" I said with a big grin as Mum resurfaced.

"Not possible!" said Mum, taking off her mask and rubbing her eyes. "I mean, you ... YOU were swimming ... for so long ... with no tank ... and..." She didn't know what to say.

It was brilliant – they were totally gobsmacked.

"Wow," Dad kept saying, over and over. "It's incredible! You really *are* Fish Kid."

After a million questions, and once they had calmed down, Mum returned to the boat. Dad and I went to collect algae for Guapo. I hoped he'd wake up soon. As soon as we were back on board, I raced in to check. I rubbed the algae across Guapo's snout, but he still didn't wake.

"He just needs more time," said Dad, patting my back. "Now you MUST tell me more about what happened. I need to know every little detail."

That's when the examination began. Being a scientist, Dad had to know exactly what was going on. He shone a light down my throat, in my eyes, up my nose and just about everywhere else, too. He studied my neck and behind my ears – looking for gills, I guess. He tested my temperature, my hearing, my sight – he even tested my wee! Forget sea cucumbers, Dad had a new test specimen.

Mum had hardly said a word. She just kept shaking her head. Dad asked question after question and wrote everything down.

As Emely and I sat with Guapo, Dad began whizzing up green smoothies.

"Is this it?" he'd ask, waving the green muck under our noses. Each time he would take a sip, then vomit it straight back into the jug. It was disgusting, but hilarious.

Dad sliced up more jellyfish and sea cucumber. He closed his eyes and held his nose as he tried to swallow bits raw. Up it came, again and again. He couldn't get a single piece down.

That night I woke up a few times to check on Guapo. He was still the same. I wondered if he'd make it till morning. Every time I got up, Dad was in the kitchen, cooking and testing. He barfed up jellyfish pancakes, sea cucumber coffee, green marshmallows and kale ice cream. He tried every concoction possible, but even after all of that, he still had no fish powers. He could only hold his breath for two minutes.

Dad woke me in the morning with more questions. I told him the powers only worked in the ocean. Dad turned and dived straight off the back of the boat. He was still in his pyjamas! And he still had no fish powers.

"Well, it's a mystery," said Dad, flopping back onto the deck. "You are some miracle, Fish Kid."

"Wait till your friends hear about this," said Mum, handing Dad a towel.

"NO!" said Dad. "We can't tell ANYONE about this."

"Huh? Why not?" I asked.

"Scientists and TV crews would be crawling all over you. You'd be locked away and tested and poked and prodded from end to end!" said Dad.

"Umm, isn't that what you've just

been doing to him, dear?" asked Mum.

"That was nothing compared to what the labs will do, trust me. And what if these powers got into the wrong hands?" Dad seemed very serious, even more so than usual.

"We must keep it a secret ... at least until we know what the secret is."

CHAPTER 19

Salty Assignment

"Marine iguanas are ectothermic. That means they use the environment to control their body temperature. They eat green algae, which is very salty. To get rid of the excess salt in their bodies, they snort it out their nostrils."

The second I read that part, Guapo snorted a salt booger! It splattered right on to my computer screen. The students all laughed. Even Mrs Snoogle giggled. I wiped the screen with my sleeve and kept going. "Because of climate change, the ocean could become too warm for algae to grow. With no food, marine iguanas like Guapo will become extinct. We all need to learn what we can do to protect our ocean and its creatures. Thank you for listening."

"Very well done," said Mrs Snoogle. The whole class clapped. Even though they were in different places, on different computers, I could see my new classmates grinning. Distance education was actually pretty cool. Everyone liked my presentation, but mostly they loved Guapo.

I closed my laptop and gave him a good scratch.

"I'm so glad he's okay," said Emely.

"Me too," I replied. Guapo climbed on to my shoulder. "Ahhhh! That hurts without a wetsuit on!" I yelped. Guapo was back to his old self now, always climbing on me!

"Hey Emely, want to go for a swim?" I asked.

"Race you!" she called, diving out the door.

We cannonballed into the water. Guapo leaped off the boat too!

"Sick bomb, Guapo!" My trusty sidekick was back. We swam around together, but not for too long. I didn't want Guapo to get cold.

After our swim, we lay on the deck,

soaking up the sunshine.

"It'd be super sad if these guys became extinct," said Emely, stroking Guapo's scaly skin.

"Yeah. I guess that's why Dad is always so serious about climate change," I said.

"Brrrrr." Emely shivered. "The ocean still feels pretty cold to me."

"Here," I said, throwing her a towel. "I'll go make us some hot chocolate."

CHAPTER 20

Payback

"PFFT!"

Salty hot chocolate spurted all over the deck. Emely was like a human fondue fountain.

"Yuck!"

A giggle snuck out from the corner of my mouth.

"YOU!" yelled the skipper's daughter. I dropped my mug and ran. Emely chased me into the ocean.

SPLASH!

"I'll get you back, Fish Kid!" yelled Emely.

I laughed and dived deep, deep down into the sparkling blue water.

THE END

About the Author

Kylie Howarth is an award-winning author and illustrator from Western Australia. She is also part fish!

Kylie has swum with whale sharks, manta rays, humpback whales, piranha, pink dolphins, lionfish, marine iguanas, hammerhead and great white sharks.

She not only draws inspiration from her underwater travels, but also from her own two fish kids who are ocean explorers too.

www.kyliehowarth.com